KNOCK!
KNOCK!
Grrr...

KNOCK!
KNOCK!

HEY, AUNT JOSEPHINE!
ARF! ARF!

For Barbara —P.S.

To Phil, Neal, and Jennifer
for bringing me along on this trio of wild rides —M.C.

Neal Porter Books

HOLIDAY HOUSE is registered in the U.S. Patent and Trademark Office.
Printed and bound in October 2020 at Leo Paper, Heshan, China.
The artwork for this book was created using pen and ink with watercolor.
www.holidayhouse.com
First Edition
1 3 5 7 9 10 8 6 4 2

Library of Congress Cataloging-in-Publication Data

Names: Stead, Philip Christian, author. | Cordell, Matthew, 1975– illustrator.
Title: Follow that frog / by Philip C. Stead ; illustrated by Matthew Cordell.
Description: New York : Holiday House, [2021] | "A Neal Porter Book."
Audience: Ages 4 to 8. | Audience: Grades 2–3. | Summary: "Aunt Josephine tells her niece Sadie the tale of her lifelong pursuit of a man-eating frog"— Provided by publisher.
Identifiers: LCCN 2020017020 | ISBN 9780823444267 (hardcover)
Subjects: CYAC: Adventure and adventurers—Fiction. | Frogs—Fiction.
Classification: LCC PZ7.S808566 Fol 2021 | DDC [E]—dc23
LC record available at https://lccn.loc.gov/2020017020

ISBN 978-0-8234-4426-7 (hardcover)

FOLLOW THAT FROG!

written by
Philip C. Stead

illustrated by
Matthew Cordell

Neal Porter Books • Holiday House • New York

KNOCK!
KNOCK!
AUNT J, WAKE UP!
ARF! ARF!

Close the curtains, Sadie! And turn out the lights!
It could be a vacuum salesman. Or more likely, a suitor.
But I tell you this! I am quite satisfied with the state of my carpets.
And my days of romance are but a memory.
I have run life's race and have earned my rest.
I have been the world over, Sadie, and today—
I will sleep past noon.

Why, by the time I was nine, my trusted canine—Orion Francis Nelson—and I were blissfully bivouacked in the jungles of Peru. We were cataloging amphibians for the scientific team of Admiral Rodriguez—who had, only recently, been lost in a tragic banana accident.

Admiral
Rodriguez

Of course, in time, my delicate beauty caught the eye of the admiral's ridiculous son. And as he stood transfixed, he was suddenly, swiftly . . .

. . . swallowed by a giant frog.

GULP!

I hollered.

For though I didn't care much for the admiral's son, I *do* abhor a job unfinished. And it was my job to catalog that frog!

STOP!
I called.

But the frog ignored my plea, instead fleeing south through the deserts of Patagonia, and onto the back of a terrified rhea—who did what any unfortunate, flightless bird would do in such a situation . . .

. . . run and run and run with no particular destination in mind.

I gave chase, northward, aboard a reluctant tortoise,
disembarking at the Panama Canal,

where the frog took a sharp left turn, heading west into tempestuous waters.

I had no choice but to catch the next available vessel, which was, by a stroke of poor luck, headed . . .

THE COMPLETELY WRONG WAY
HONG KONG
ROME
NAIROBI
NEW ORLEANS
KALAMAZOO
PARIS
ADELAIDE

I chose to stay positive, though, remembering the last words of my sainted grandmother:

And I would have . . .

. . . if not for pirates off the coasts of the Canary Islands,
who commandeered my humble ship, leaving me to wonder:
Exactly how many canaries does it take to make an island?

A great many, I concluded!

Are you sure I shouldn't get the door, Aunt J?

Quite sure, Sadie, yes. And now
I have a question for you:
Have you ever ridden a whale?
Well, I hadn't either,
but—guess what?—
it's not unlike riding a horse! All you
need are a few encouraging words—

GIDDYUP!
YEEHAW!

FOLLOW THAT FROG!

But of course a whale goes where a whale goes. And while we were many months at sea and a long way from Paris, I made the best of our adventure—

taking in the sights, but never losing sight of the goal.

Now, Sadie, after all these years and all the places I've been, I am tired. I have but one regret. For one day, Sadie, you and I will see Paris . . .

KNOCK!
KNOCK!
ARF!
ARF!

. . . but I may never, ever find that frog.

Well, Aunt J, there's always hope.

KNOCK! KNOCK!
POST